P9-CQE-138

Three Little Kittens

For Jamie, Jacob, Nathaniel, and Mariska

Copyright © 1986 Paul Galdone

All rights reserved. Published in the United States by HMH Books, an imprint of Houghton Mifflin Harcourt Publishing Company. Originally published in hardcover in the United States by Clarion Books, an imprint of Houghton Mifflin Harcourt Publishing Company, 1986.

HMH Books and the HMH Books logo are trademarks of Houghton Mifflin Harcourt Publishing Company.

For information about permission to reproduce selections from this book, write to trade.permissions@hmhco.com or to Permissions, Houghton Mifflin Harcourt Publishing Company, 3 Park Avenue, 19th Floor, New York, New York 10016.
www.hmhco.com

The Library of Congress Cataloging-in-Publication data is on file.

ISBN: 978-0-89919-426-4 hardcover
ISBN: 978-0-89919-796-8 paperback
ISBN: 978-0-547-57575-9 paper over board

Manufactured in China
LEO 10 9 8 7 6 5
4500612325

Three Little Kittens

A Folk Tale Classic

Illustrated by

PAUL GALDONE

Houghton Mifflin Harcourt
Boston New York

Three

R0447839224

"Oh, Mother Dear, we sadly fear
Our mittens we have lost!"

CATNIP
chopped
minced
blended
ground
Seed
roots
leaves
FLOU

"What! lost your mittens,
you naughty kittens!
FLOU

Then you shall have no pie."

"Meow, meow, meow,
Meow, meow, meow, meow!"

The three little kittens

found their mittens
and they began to cry,

"Oh! Mother Dear, see here, see here.
Our mittens we have found."

"What!
found your mittens,
you good little kittens,

purrrrr...
purrrr.
purrr

Then
you shall
have
some pie."
"Purr,
purr,
purr."

The three little kittens

put on their mittens
and soon ate up the pie.

"Oh! Mother Dear, we greatly fear
Our mittens we have soiled."

"What! soiled your mittens,
you naughty kittens!"

Then they
began to sigh,
"Meow,
meow,
meow!"

The three little kittens

washed their mittens,

and hung them up to dry.

"Oh! Mother Dear,
look here, look here,

Our mittens
we have
washed."

"What! washed your mittens,
you darling kittens!

But
hush!
I smell
a rat
close
by."

"Yes, we smell a rat close by.
Meow, meow, *meow!*"